THE ASTONISHING ADVENTURES

OF THE DASHING AND VALIANT

BOY PRODIGIES

MADDOX & TRISTAN

STORY BY MADDOX KRUSE & TRISTAN BLAKEMAN

WRITTEN BY LINDSEY PHERSON

PUBLISHED BY DC PRESS

DC PRESS

www.dcpressbooks.org

CHAPTER ONE

Fearsome Boney Blaze and Fiery Fatality

Maddox "Mad Jack" Kruse and Tristan "Tritch" Blakeman were two ordinary boys like you. That is, until they met James on the beach that day and their ordinary lives changed forever.

It was a beautiful, sunny day on the quiet, peaceful village of Port Scanty, a lovely place in the Woeful Islands on the dazzling and balmy Caribbean Sea.

On that day, that very special day, these two ordinary boys were playing together on the beach, as they did every day they weren't in their small, one room school house learning math, science, reading and all about the world around them to become smart and well educated.

The boys were both tall for their age and blonde, and they wore long, black jackets, wide black hats with red feathers on the brim and scabbards on their belts.

They were thought to be the most handsome boys on the Woeful Islands, but their mothers always said they needed to be smart and well-educated as well as handsome in order to become good men.

But Maddox and Tristan preferred sword fighting and playing on the beach to learning about stars, nations, literature and arithmetic.

The two boys loved sword fighting above all things, and they were the best sword fighters on the Woeful Islands, even though they were both only eight.

They had been training since before they could walk, and then they would use their wooden swords to battle each other from their cribs and in their rolling walkers.

Their poor mothers were beside themselves, afraid their two boys would hurt each other or cut their own heads right off!

So their mothers insisted that their sons train well and become the best fighters on the island.

Then they would never have to be worried about them or be in danger from the many pirates who attacked the Woeful villages and stole all the villagers' gold and jewels to become rich while the poor, desperate villagers starved.

On that day, the special day we mentioned already, Mad Jack and Tritch were practicing their skills on the beach, their swords glinting in the sun, whooshing and reverberating as they swung them through the air and clanged them together.

Little did they know that in a few short moments, their amazing and renowned fighting skills and all the things they learned in their one room school house would be put to the test.

Maddox swung his sword with a loud and terrible war cry.

The boys always liked to make the loudest war cries they could when they were fighting because their mothers didn't let them shout and scream in the house.

They had to be quiet in school so that they didn't disturb the other children who wanted to learn. So when they were on the beach practicing their sword fighting, they made all the noise they wanted.

Maddox swung his sword at his friend, but it didn't clank against Tristan's.

It whooshed powerfully through the air and sliced through the sand with a sharp snick.

He blinked in surprise and looked up at Tristan.

Tristan stood perfectly still, staring out over the sea with his hand cupped over his eyes to block the glare of the high late morning sun that glittered down across the sand.

Tristan lifted his other hand to point into the distance.

"Hey, Mad Jack, look there."

Maddox dropped his sword hand to his side and strode to stand beside his best friend.

"What is it?" he asked.

"It looks like a schooner."

Tristan was right.

It was a schooner, and it was zipping so quickly across the water toward Port Scanty that the boys were afraid it might crash!

"Oh, no!" Maddox exclaimed.

He lifted his sword to point out at the horizon beyond the speedy schooner.

"There's another ship coming after it."

They looked past the schooner, and they were shocked at what they saw.

It was not the first time they had seen a ship, but this ship was huge and menacing.

Its hull was rusty red, the paint peeling off its sides as though the salt of the sea had been scuffing and weathering it for many, many years.

Its sails were dark and holey, but the ship sliced across the water with unnatural speed, as though it was moved by magic or the water itself and needed no wind to sail.

A huge, black ratty flag hung on main mast, fluttering in the balmy tropical breeze.

As the ship drew closer, the boys could see the image emblazoned on the flag.

It was a grinning skeleton brandishing a bloody, rusty sword.

It wore a pirate hat with the top cut off. Flames blazed from out of the top of the hat.

On the side of the ship, the words Fiery Fatality were painted in jagged black letters.

It was a terrifying, ominous sight, but the boys were not afraid; they were brave and daring, and they did not fear pirates, for they were the best fighters on the Woeful Islands.

The Fiery Fatality and the small schooner raced toward the shore.

They were sure to crash!

The schooner banked against the shore, and a tall man with dark hair leapt out onto the glittering white sand.

His clothes were torn and dirty, and his face was streaked with soot.

He looked as though he had been living rough on the uninhabited islands for many days.

He probably smelled very bad, too, but the boys were not worried about that. His expression was urgent.

Maddox and Tristan knew who he was. His name was James, and he lived in Port Scanty in a small shell cottage near the shore.

They didn't know him well, for he spent much of his time traveling around the world on adventures.

They liked James. They wanted to be like him when they got older, using their education and skills to have grand, exciting adventures around the Caribbean Sea, searching for treasure or discovering sunken ships.

James was carrying a scroll of paper in his hand. When he saw the boys standing on the shore with their swords at their sides, he spun and raced toward them.

He knew they were the best fighters on the island, and he knew that they had been learning about the world in school since they were very young. They were his only hope!

"Mad Jack! Tritch!"

They ran to meet him. "What's happening, James?" Maddox asked. "Why are those pirates chasing you?"

"They want this." He pressed the scroll into Maddox's hand. "You have to take it. You have to keep it safe and find the treasure."

"Treasure?"

James looked behind him. The Fiery Fatality had reached the island and was sliding up onto the sandy shore.

"Quickly, boys!" he said frantically.

Maddox handed Tristan the scroll of paper, which was a map to a magnificent treasure that the pirates wanted all for themselves, even though they hadn't earned it.

Tristan always kept things safe.

He tucked the map into the secret pocket on the inside of his long, black jacket with lots of big, brass buttons down the front.

"Go!" James ordered.

The boys glanced toward the pirate ship. What they saw was horrifying.

An army of skeletons marched along the quarter deck like caged jungle animals hungry to eat the little boys and girls who poked their fingers at them through the bars at the zoo.

They were dressed like pirates, but their clothes hung loosely on their bones, as they had no skin to hold it up.

They all carried large, rusty swords, which they brandished menacingly at James and the boys.

They didn't talk like normal people, but they made a strange, harmonic sound like a long, continuous death rattle deep in their hollow chests.

A man stood on the bridge of the terrifying Fiery Fatality, and he was more terrifying still than even the ship or the skeleton pirate army alighting on the sparkling shore.

He, too, was a great skeleton, but he was dressed grandly like a king in a long, red velvet jacket with buttons down the front and sharp metal spikes jutting out from the shoulders.

His eyes glowed the bright, electric blue of hottest fire. Red, blue and orange flames shot out of the top of the wide-brimmed black hat he wore atop his grinning skull head, just like the skeleton on the flag!

A red head band, the exact color of blood, wrapped around his bleached, boney forehead.

The captain of the Fiery Fatality was called Fearsome Boney Blaze, but his crew called him "Your Majesty" as though he was a king, but he wasn't.

He was just a wicked, greedy pirate whose skin had long since rotted away and whose eyes were nothing more than licks of blue flame.

He was feared by all across the Woeful Islands and the Caribbean Sea, for he was as ruthless and terrible as any pirate and it was said that he could never be killed, even with a sword and a gun.

Maddox and Tristan had heard tales of Fearsome Boney Blaze, but they were not afraid, for they were valiant and courageous.

They raised their swords and prepared to fight the skeletons that were coming right at them, rattling horribly as though they were struggling to take their last breath.

"No, boys," James said bravely.

He drew his sword and brandished it at the skeletons racing toward them through the white, gleaming sand.

"I will fight them. You must go quickly! Take my schooner. Follow the map to the treasure. It is the only way to save our village from starvation and poverty!"

"What about you?" Maddox demanded. "We cannot leave you to the pirate skeletons!"

"I will be fine." James faced the skeletons fearlessly.

"I know how to fight them," he added. "I am afraid they will follow you, so you must be careful and watch behind you. You are the best fighters in the village and have learned much in school. You are the only ones who can do this."

The boys did not want to leave James alone to fight the skeletons.

It seemed cowardly, and the boys were not cowards.

But they knew they must go, and so they raced toward James' schooner as the skeletons approached with uncanny speed toward James.

James was not as good a fighter as Maddox and Tristan, but he whipped his sword through the air as the skeletons reached them.

Their bones broke apart as his sword struck them and landed in heaps at his feet.

None of them struck him, for he was much quicker and they seemed unnaturally easy to break.

Maddox turned back as the army of skeletons descended on James like a swarm of gnats. "We should stay and help him!"

"No," Tristan said firmly. "We can't! We have to get the treasure."

He grabbed Maddox's arm and tugged him toward the schooner.

"Come on!"

They raced toward the battered wooden schooner and with a great heave they pushed it into the water and leapt into the deck.

The boat shot out across the glassy, brilliant blue water.

Behind them, Fearsome Boney Blaze was making an awful, ghastly din.

They turned back to see the heaps of skeletons bones rattling.

Suddenly, the bones sprung up into the air and formed back into the hideous, sun-bleached skeleton pirates as though they'd never been broken apart at all!

The skeleton army raced back to their captain, as though the noise he was making was some sort of horrendous call to arms.

"Uh, oh," Tristan said.

The skeletons clambered back onto the deck of the Fiery Fatality, leaving James standing alone on the shore.

James cupped his hands around his mouth.

They heard his voice shouting at them, but the ocean breeze carried the words away before they could reach the boys.

"Tritch, look!"

Maddox lifted his finger to point, and they knew what James had been shouting at them.

The Fiery Fatality had spun around and was in hot pursuit of the schooner!

"Hurry!" Tristan ordered. "We have to be faster! We must get away from them."

"Which way do I go?"

Tristan tugged the map out of his jacket pocket and spread it out on the deck before him. He stood and looked up at the sun and spun around him.

He pointed out toward the left. "That way!"

Maddox trusted Tristan's navigation skills, for he was not only one of the best fighters but a very good navigator, as well.

Maddox yanked the helm and the boat spun wildly around, skipping across the water.

They turned toward the sun and sped away, leaving the Fiery Fatality behind as they sailed out, away from Port Scanty and their home on the Woeful Islands.

CHAPTER TWO

Bonny Bertha and Kismet Island

The schooner bobbed serenely across the calm, still water. A gentle, salty breeze carried it further and further east, toward the important mission on which James had sent them.

He had not left them without the proper provisions.

There was a stash of dried fruit, nuts and meat in a small, metal box that looked as though it had spent much time floating across the water, for schooners often capsized and one must protect their belongings so they don't sink or float away.

After several hours on the wide, endless expanse of sea, the boys sat down to nibble on the food James had left them.

They did not know when next they would have the opportunity to find a meal, so they ate sparingly and saved the rest for later.

As they ate, they stared out toward the horizon.

There was nothing to see but the sea and the fluffy white clouds floating above, barely high enough to obscure the bright, dazzling sun and protect their eyes, for they had no chance to grab their sunglasses. They had to cover their eyes with their hands to block the glare.

"Which way should we go next?" Maddox asked, leaning back against the wall of the boat with his feet up.

He loved the open sea, and he was enjoying the sun beating down on his face and the smell of the salt water around them.

Tristan studied the map.

"The treasure is hidden somewhere on Swag Island."

He glanced down at the small, brass compass above the helm. Its needle pointed north.

"We need to go northeast."

Maddox nodded and rose to take the large, wooden wheel that steered the boat. He spun it right, and the boat zipped across the water.

"Whose treasure do you think it is?"

"There is a story on the back of the map. It says the treasure belonged to a pirate queen called Bonny Bertha the Bold. She fell in love with a villager from the islands, but he did not love her because he already had a family of his own at home.

"But he tricked her into giving him the map to his treasure by telling her he loved her when he didn't."

"That's a nasty trick."

"It's not a very nice thing to do. Not even for treasure."

"He should be ashamed of himself."

Tristan looked back at the story on the back of the map.

"He was ashamed, for he never looked for the treasure, and he apologized for lying to her."

"That was the right thing to do."

"Yes. Both Bonny Bertha and the villager died many years ago, and he left the map to his son."

"Why didn't his son seek the treasure?"

"The map was obtained through trickery and deceit. Perhaps he felt as though he had no right to the treasure."

They thought about this in silence for a moment. "Do we have any right to the treasure?"

"We did not obtain the map through lying and stealing. The rightful owners are long gone now. It is the only way to save our villages from starvation, so finding and using it is the right thing to do."

Tristan peered down at the map.

"There is note from James that finishes the story. He heard about Bonny Bertha's treasure and went to the villager's son to ask him to give him the map to save the Woeful Islands.

"The villager's son was ashamed of his father's artifice and did not look for the treasure. He gave James the map so the islands could be wealthy and have food again."

Maddox nodded as he thought about this.

"It was wrong for the villager to trick the pirate queen, even though the treasure wasn't hers to begin with, but we will use it for good, and maybe the villager can feel better about what he did to Bertha."

"How will he know we're using it for good?"

"I think he will see."

Tristan peered pensively up at the sky. Finally, he nodded.

"I hope he does. It would be terrible to feel ashamed for all of eternity."

"Yes." Suddenly, Maddox stood straight up and pointed in excitement. "I see land! Is it Swag Island?"

Tristan clambered up to the deck and leaned over the side to squint into the sun ahead. There was an island there, a small, bright copse of green trees just ahead in the distance.

He looked at the compass and back down at the map.

"No, I don't think so. It's a different island. It could be Kismet Island or one of the Carcass Isles between the Woeful Islands and Swag Islands. We will have to go around it."

Maddox sighed, for he was getting bored out on the water and would have appreciated a good treasure hunt. He had learned patience, however, and he did not complain.

He turned the wheel to avoid Kismet Island, but what he saw in the distance shocked him so that his insides turned to ice. "Oh, no!"

The Fiery Fatality was approaching on the horizon so swiftly across the water, Maddox had to spin the helm so they would not collide with it. He steeled his nerves and looked at his best friend with a grim expression.

Tristan was already on his feet. "Should we fight them?"

Maddox did not wish to run from a fight, but their village was starving. They did not have time to battle the pirates.

"We have to get away. James sent us to save our village, not scuffle with skeleton pirate kings."

Tristan nodded, though he, too, wished they could stay and stand up to the Fiery Fatality. "We are smaller and faster. We can outrun them."

The Fiery Fatality, however, was unnaturally fast. In moments, it drew up beside them as though the pirates intended to leap overboard into the small schooner's deck.

"Tristan!" Maddox shouted. He drew his sword and prepared to fight.

The skeleton pirates were making that ghastly rattling noise that would have chilled the blood of less courageous men and boys than Maddox and Tristan.

The boys stood their ground as the rattling grew into a terrible crescendo that crashed over them like a wave.

The skeletons lined the deck of the Fiery Fatality in a jangling row. They held bottles of dark amber liquid in their boney hands.

Behind them, Fearsome Boney Blaze bent his head, and his crew raised their bottles to the flames that crackled and spit through the top of his hat.

The bottles ignited into deadly, flaming projectiles, for, though most pirates loved rum, skeletons did not drink alcohol, and so they used their rum as weapons.

This did not bode well for the brave boys, as, though they were great and daring fighters, their schooner was still made of wood and would light up like a flimsy match if the skeleton's fiery projectiles were to strike it.

"Hit them in the air!" Maddox suggested, raising his sword to meet the flying bottles.

"It will do no good! They will be too close, and the glass might cut us or the flaming liquid will hit the schooner!" Tristan replied.

A barrage of flaming bottles sailed through the air toward them.

"They are trying to sink our boat!" Maddox said.

They tried to swat the flying bottles with their swords, for it was their only hope, but Tristan had been right. The shards of broken bottle glass showered them, and they covered their heads to protect their faces.

The glass bounced off the thick velvet of their jackets, but they could not withstand the assault indefinitely.

A bottle struck the main sail of the schooner, and it lit up in a fiery blaze.

"Oh, no!" Maddox exclaimed, waving his sword to fend off the attack, but there were too many skeletons with bottles of plundered rum and other spirits, and more of the projectiles struck the small boat.

Fire spread across the floor of the boat, and the boys leapt backward to avoid it.

"We have to get away or we will sink and they will take the map!" Tristan said, dancing from one foot to the other to avoid the spreading flames.

"What do skeletons need with treasure?"

"They are pirates. What else do they want but treasure?"

"It seems a little silly to me. They can't even do anything with it! They're dead!"

"Well, that Fearsome Boney Blaze sure looks like he wants it."

"What are we going to do?" Maddox asked.

"We have to jump and swim to shore! It's the only way."

Maddox did not like this idea, but he knew they would never escape the Fiery Fatality in their blazing boat.

"Okay! I'm ready!"

"Jump!"

In the same moment, they leapt into the water. It was warm on the surface from the beating sun, but cold water sucked at their boots as they sunk under the schooner's and the Fiery Fatality's waves.

They kicked with their heavy boots and shot back up to the surface. They took deep breaths and looked at each other.

They nodded at each other, for they both knew what they must do.

The boys had learned to swim almost before they'd learned to walk, for they lived on an island and loved the beach more than any place in the world. They were very good swimmers, and they swam so fast, the Fiery Fatality could barely keep up.

The schooner blazed and burned behind them, but they did not turn back. They could still hear the skeletons rattling, and the king keening hideously at their backs.

They did not stop for anything!

When they washed up on the sandy, sun-beaten shores of Kismet Island, they were exhausted and their eyes stung from the smoke of the fires and the salt of the sea.

They rolled over onto their backs, gasping for breath as the sun warmed them and dried their long, black jackets.

Suddenly, though, the Fiery Fatality caught up to them, barreling inexorably toward Kismet Island's shore.

"Oh, no!" Maddox exclaimed, sitting up to point urgently at the pirate ship. "They're already here!"

Tristan leapt to his feet, tugging on his best friend's arm. "Run!"

They did, and they ran so fast, the uncannily speedy skeleton pirates could barely keep up with them, let alone catch them.

The wicked, rattling pirates didn't give up, though. They chased the boys over the sand, waving their swords in the air.

"They're gaining on us!" Maddox shouted.

"Keep going! We'll find a way to escape them."

And, in a moment, they did. "Tritch, look! I think I see a cave!"

A large, grey outcropping of rock lined the sand around the island. The stones were nearly twice as tall as the boys, and they were as jagged and sharp as twisted metal. One of the rocks rose higher than the others, and a large, black cave mouth yawned widely as if to invite them in.

The boys poked their heads carefully into the mouth. The jagged rocks seemed to almost form teeth, and there was nothing to see in the endless, stygian dark.

They weren't afraid of the uncertainty of the dark; the boys had never been afraid of the dark, not since they were tiny boys.

They stepped carefully into the inky darkness.

Tristan had a couple flashlights in his pocket, for he was always prepared, and handed one to Maddox.

"We should go further in. Those pirates might see the light from the cave mouth," Maddox told him.

"Good thinking. But we should block off the entrance. We don't want them to get in after us. We don't know if we'll get trapped here inside."

"There are some big rocks over here. If we work together, we can push one in front of the entrance and conceal the cave from the pirates."

"Let's do it."

The two boys were very strong, as they had spent so much time in training and swords fighters must have strength as well as skill and speed.

Together, they managed to push a large, flat rock in front of the gaping cave mouth.

As soon as they did, the meager light from the beach beyond the cave mouth blinked out completely. The boys stood in absolute darkness.

They flipped on their flashlights. The pale, yellow beams of light barely illuminated the darkness, but they could see the walls around them and the few feet ahead. Tristan cast his light around at the rounded stone walls at their sides and above their heads.

"There is writing on these walls," he said keenly. "Look, Mad Jack."

Maddox turned his light to examine the small symbols scratched onto the walls with sticks or a small, sharp knife. "They look like hieroglyphs."

Maddox and Tristan knew about hieroglyphics because they had learned about them in school. A long time ago, civilizations had used the small pictures to represent words to make sentences. Some countries still used them.

"Do you know what they say?"

"No. I have never seen this language before. But they must be pretty old. People haven't used hieroglyphs to communicate on the islands in many years."

Tristan liked to learn new things because the more he learned, the more he knew, and he the more he knew, the smarter he became.

He wanted to be the smartest person on the Woeful Islands. Aside from his best friend, Maddox, of course.

He wanted Maddox to be smart too because they could talk together about the interesting things they had learned all day long.

"Wow. I wish I had a camera or some paper or something. I would like to know what the words mean," he said.

"Me, too," Maddox replied, "but I don't think we have time to copy them. Do you hear that?"

What Maddox heard was the skeleton's ghastly death rattle outside the cave mouth. They didn't seem to be able to get in, but they knew the boys were inside the cave.

They sure hoped they could get out somehow. The pirates would be waiting for them if they had to go out the way they came in.

"The only way to go is forward."

Maddox nodded resolutely. "Let's go."

There were more interesting pictures on the walls as they went: paintings of kings on thrones surrounded by their loyal subjects; large jungle cats with blood-stained fangs attacking warriors who fended them off with spears; and two boys who looked very much like themselves bathed in radiant sunlight, sitting upon piles and piles of gold.

They liked that picture, but they didn't have time to study the paintings more closely, even though they wanted to.

They wondered what other fascinating things were in the cave.

"Look at the ground, Mad Jack," Tristan said.

Maddox turned his flashlight to the cave floor at his feet. "What are they?"

Tristan bent down and poked his finger through the debris. "It looks like pieces of broken pottery. Oh, no."

"What is it?"

"Bones."

"There are bones on the ground?"

Maddox stepped forward to flash his light at the floor, and what he saw chilled his blood.

Without even realizing it, the boys had tromped over the stone floor and now stood on a large pile of bones. The bones were so old they had fossilized and were as hard and heavy as rock.

"Not just bones," Tristan said. "Fossils."

"That's bad, isn't it?"

Tristan wasn't sure if it was bad; fossils were very interesting.

And then, the bones started to shake.

"Whoa!" Maddox said, jumping to his left in surprise, but the whole floor was so covered in the bones, he couldn't get away from the trembling ground.

"What's going on?" Tristan demanded.

They backed up toward the cave mouth from which they had come and turned back around just in time to see the bones start to fly up into the air like the pirates' had done.

Suddenly, the bones sprung together to make shapes.

The shapes weren't strictly human shapes, for some of them had legs for arms and arms for legs and skulls for hands and hands for toes and fingers for heads and some of them even had five skulls all stacked up for a leg.

The weird and hideous bones made the same horrible death rattling noise as the skeletons waiting for them outside. They were a strange, mismatched army, but they were as dangerous as any normal shaped army.

The boys drew their swords and struck the skeleton soldiers as they converged upon them.

The bones broke apart as easily as the pirates', but as soon as they did, they rolled across the floor to join another solider bodies until some of them grew so huge with six legs and ten arms and twenty skulls and hundreds of fingers and toes.

"I think we're in trouble, Tristan!" Maddox said, slicing his sword through the air to topple a pile of bones so high, it could have reached the roof of the cave if it had only lifted its arm, which was really three legs. "We have to get out of this cave!"

"But the pirates are waiting at the entrance! There's no way out!"

"We will have to fight our way through them. It's better than staying here and fighting these guys until we're too tired. It isn't a good option, but it's the best one."

"Okay. I'm not afraid."

The boys turned and hurried back the way they came. They were tired from the fighting, but they were still strong and knew they had to keep going if they were to get away.

They pushed the heavy rock door away from the cave mouth.

The skeleton pirates streamed into the cave entrance, shrieking that terrible, rattling war cry. Maddox and Tristan sliced and struck and fought their way through the center of the angry swarm.

Bones flew out in every direction.

They stepped out onto the beach, gasping for breath, for even the best of fighters cannot fight indefinitely with no food, water or rest.

Fearsome Boney Blaze was waiting for them. He grinned his skeleton grin and flashed his flaming blue eyes at the boys.

Behind them, the boys felt the skeleton pirates and the motley army from the cave seize their arms, legs, clothes and everything they could touch.

Captain Blaze laughed a smug, wicked laugh. "Arr! Take these boys back to the Fiery Fatality! I have a bone to pick with them."

CHAPTER THREE

The Triumph of Mad Jack and Tritch

Maddox woke up first and looked around the tiny cell in the brig of the Fiery Fatality. There was barely enough room for he and Tristan to stretch out their legs.

His wrists were tied behind his back with a length of rough rope, and he glanced over to see his best friend slumped over, still sleeping from the punching the skeletons had given them as they dragged them up from the glittering shores of Kismet Island to the ship.

Tristan's hands were tied, too.

Hanging from the bars around them, as though the prisoners had slumped over in exhaustion with their arms reaching for freedom, were several skeletons.

Their clothes, the remnants of their pirate garb, hung off them in rags.

Maddox eyed them warily for a long moment, but they gave no indication that they were part of the ship's crew.

They did not move or make any horrible rattling noises.

They just hung there silently.

Outside the bars, though, a line of skeleton pirates stood guard with their backs to the prisoners. They did not notice yet that Maddox had awakened. He didn't want to draw their attention, but he needed to wake his friend.

He wasn't entirely sure they could speak or hear anything, though they did make noise and Fearsome Boney Blaze could speak, even though his voice sounded like fire crackling in a brazier.

"Tritch," he hissed. He nudged Tristan. "Wake up."

Tristan stirred and moaned a little. Maddox looked anxiously up at the guards, but they did not seem to notice. Maddox nudged Tristan again.

Finally, Tristan lifted his head and blinked blearily at Maddox. "What is it? Where are we?"

"On the Fiery Fatality," Maddox whispered. "We were captured, remember?"

Tristan sighed. "Yes, I remember. How are we ever going to save our village if we get captured right away?"

"We will save the village. We have to. We will find a way." Maddox looked out at the guards, but none of them seemed to realize that the boys were awake.

They did not turn back to them. Nevertheless, Maddox whispered in the quietest voice he could, "Do you have the map?"

"Yes. They must have looked for it because my clothes are all twisted up, but I hid it in my special pocket."

Maddox knew which pocket he was talking about.

This special pocket had been a gift from the village sorcerer, Kiki, who had sewed it into the jacket as a reward for saving his prized parakeet from a nasty old cat.

It was a magical pocket, and no one but Tristan could open it--unless he was in trouble, and then Maddox could get inside to help him.

"Do you have anything in there that could get us out of this?"

Tristan wiggled around for a moment. "My arms are tied."

"Mine, too."

Outside the bars, the skeletons started rattling. The boys' pulses leapt. The skeletons had realized they were awake, and they were keening noisily.

The boys knew what that meant; they were calling Fearsome Boney Blaze, and he was coming quickly.

He stood before them with his head aflame, and his eyes flickering as though even the fire in his skull was filled with rage. His skeleton mouth grinned, but he still looked terrible and angry.

He just stood there for several seconds, staring at them. They didn't know if his fire eyes could see them, but he seemed to be glaring menacingly at them.

He carried a large stick, which looked burnt and jagged at the tip like a spear that had been set aflame many times. It probably had.

The flames in his head rose and crackled and popped as though they grew with his anger.

"Yarr!" he growled, and the skeletons around him jangled and rattled. "I be wanting that map in your pocket, matey, and if ye not be giving it to me, 'twill be your heads!"

Captain Blaze reached up and touched the stick to his fiery head. The tip ignited in wicked blue flame. He jabbed it through the bars at the boys.

On its way, the flaming stick brushed the hanging, ragged sleeve of one of the skeleton prisoners. It smoked and hissed before it snuffed out.

The heat of the fire set sweat dribbling down the boys' foreheads, and they leaned back to avoid it. "What do we do?" Maddox whispered.

Tristan had been squirming around for some time, and now all his effort had paid off. A knife slid out of his special pocket and clanked on the salty wooden floor.

He leaned to the side and scooped it up. He sliced it quickly through his bonds.

Fearsome Boney Blaze jabbed his flaming poker at Maddox's face. Maddox leaned back as far as he could, but the cell was smaller than the stick.

It was sure to burn him!

But Tristan was quicker. He cut Maddox's ropes, and Maddox dove out of the way of the poker just in time.

"Yarr!" Fearsome Boney Blaze snarled. "No! I be wanting that treasure map!"

Maddox and Tristan didn't have their swords. They were strapped to the skeleton guards' belts for safe keeping, for the pirates knew the boys were very skilled with their weapons and didn't want to take any risks.

The boys needed to get their swords back if they were to battle this crew of rattling skeleton pirates!

They looked at each other meaningfully. They knew what they must do. They jumped to their feet, and as Fearsome Boney Blaze opened the cage to get to them, they ran at him and shoved him backward into his crew with all their strength.

He stumbled, and his crewmen scrambled to catch him before he fell to the ground and broke apart.

The captain shouted in anger, but the boys dove for their swords while the pirates were distracted by their captain's plight.

They grabbed the guns out of their holsters for good measure, too, because sometimes you need a gun to fight a pirate, especially when they have guns of their own!

They used their swords to slash and jab at the crew. The skeletons broke apart and crumpled to the floor.

The others scuttled away to avoid the boys' blades, but none were spared the fate of their brothers, and the pile of bones began to rise around Captain Blaze, who snarled and shouted for his crew to capture the boys.

Soon, there were none left in the brig but the captain, who was so buried under the pile of scattered bones, they could barely hear him cursing and shouting at them as he struggled to dig himself out.

The boys raced up the stairs onto the bright, sunlit deck.

There were more pirates on the deck, moving about on their rounds and duties, but they spun in a single, choreographed movement as the boys popped up unexpectedly from the brig.

They keened and rattled and pointed with their swords.

"Uh, oh! We'll have to fight our way out," Maddox said bravely. He nodded to Tristan and the boys raised their swords.

They both let out a blood-curdling war cry and rushed forward, slashing and slicing.

They broke the skeletons apart, one by one. Bones flew in every direction. Tristan scooped up a pile of bones and shouted to Maddox.

"Toss them overboard! They won't be able to go back together!"

"Good thinking!"

The boys ran around the ship, scooping up the bones and tossing them over the side of the ship into the churning sea below. But by then, the pirates from the brig had joined back together, and more pirates came at them in a seemingly inexorable horde.

They fought them off with their swords and shot them with their guns, and then they threw their bones overboard so they couldn't keep coming anymore. It was exhaustive work!

The pirates just kept coming as though there were hundreds and hundreds of them all over the ship, just waiting to spring alive and attack the two boys.

While Tristan battled the skeletons on the deck of the ship, Maddox clambered swiftly up the main mast to the black crow's nest, from which he could look down at the fight below.

He aimed his gun carefully at a line of skeletons charging toward Tristan and knocked them all down with one shot.

The bones blew apart into several directions. Tristan looked up at Maddox and grinned. Maddox raised his gun above his head in triumph, then took aim again and fired at more of the skeletons as they rushed at his friend.

Tristan had his hands full with the rest of the crew, and he was slicing and slashing in a wild frenzy as bones flew all around him. The battle raged on and on for many minutes and seemed as though it might never end.

Then Fearsome Boney Blaze marched up onto the deck. The fire in his skull shot so high, it nearly ignited the sails above his head.

He looked so angry, the fire might shoot out at them--even Maddox, who was really, really high up!

He carried a bottle of amber liquid, which he raised to his flaming head. It lit up like a torch.

"You'll sink your own ship!" Maddox shouted at him from the crow's nest, but Blaze probably didn't hear him over the sounds of battle and the crackling of his own flames.

Anyway, it didn't seem as if he cared that his ship might sink. He tossed the bottle up at the main mast without any regard for his ship.

The crew was dead, and they probably didn't care if they drowned.

Maddox and Tristan did, though. They could not sink to the ocean floor and rise back up without a worry in the world. They wouldn't survive.

Maddox aimed his gun and fired as fast as lightning at the blazing bottle as it flew toward him and the sail. It shattered into thousands of tiny pieces and splashed into the ocean before it could do any harm.

But Fearsome Boney Blaze wasn't finished. He had dozens and dozens of those bottles, for if pirates had anything, it was lots and lots of rum and lots and lots of ill-gotten gains.

He tossed the bottles wildly into the air, almost too quickly for Maddox to shoot.

Tristan pulled out his gun and fired at the flaming flying bottles. They exploded in the air and showered licks of flame down on the skeleton pirates.

Their clothes ignited, but they still fought relentlessly.

Tristan didn't give up, though, and while Maddox fired at the flaming bottles flying around the sails, Tristan determinedly battled the horde.

Finally, they lay in a huge pile of bones at his feet, and Fearsome Boney Blaze was the only pirate left on the deck.

And he was mad. Tristan leapt toward him to fight, but the heat from his blazing head was too intense to get too close.

He drew his own sword and brandished it at Tristan.

Maddox saw that his friend was in trouble, and he climbed quickly down the main mast to stand beside him with his sword raised.

They both let out their terrible battle cry as the captain keened in fury.

The boys rushed to meet Captain Blaze as he charged at them, swinging his rusty, bloody sword with such power, they were nearly thrown backwards from the force of his strike.

They met his blade with their own, and a fierce battle raged for several moments on the Fiery Fatality's bone-scattered deck.

Captain Blaze was a very good fighter, and the heat from his skull was intense, but the boys were better fighters.

They sliced and slashed with their swords and fired their guns with their other hands.

Fearsome Boney Blaze jerked and staggered as the bullets hit him.

The king scooped up bits of bone and debris from the deck, which he ignited with his head and tossed at them.

The boys evaded them swiftly, but the bones, rags and wood on the floor lit up, and fire spread across the deck.

Finally, Maddox and Tristan aimed their guns at the same time, and they blew the Captain's flaming head right off!

It landed in a puddle of water on the deck and the fire sizzled and hissed as it snuffed out. The boys sighed in relief.

"Hurry!" Tristan said. "Throw the bones overboard. We don't want to have to fight them all over again."

"No, we don't," Maddox agreed earnestly.

They scooped up all the bones and threw them over the sides of the boat into the water. Then they pulled buckets of water up to the deck to put out the fires Boney Blaze had so carelessly started on his own ship.

After that, they went down into the brig to collect the rest of the bones and toss them overboard.

"Should we throw the prisoners over, too?" Tristan asked. "It seems a little heartless."

"They died sad deaths, but we cannot risk our lives to protect their bones. What if they come to life and try to attack us?"

Tristan nodded. "Just to be safe."

And so they threw the prisoner's bones overboard, too, and when all the bones, even the Fearsome Boney Blaze's smoldering head, were scattered in the roiling waves, the boys turned and grinned at each other.

The Fiery Fatality belonged to them now.

Maddox strode triumphantly for the bridge and stood at the helm. "Which way, navigator?"

Tristan pulled out the map and checked the compass. "Do north, Captain."

The sun was just beginning to set as Maddox spun the wheel north, and they set out toward Swag Island.

CHAPTER FOUR

The Kraken

The boys sailed happily toward Swag Island under the bright sun. It was a warm and balmy day. Maddox steered the Fiery Fatality, which they had decided to rename the Triumph of Mad Jack and Tritch.

Tristan leaned lazily over the side of the ship with his chin on his hand, peering out at the endless expanse of sea ahead.

He squinted in the sun. "I think I see something ahead."

Maddox perked up. "Land?"

"No. I'm not sure what it is. It looks like something else. The water is darker over there."

Maddox frowned over at where Tristan was pointing. "What do you think it is?"

"I'm not sure."

"Should I keep going or try to avoid it?"

Tristan frowned thoughtfully. "We can avoid it. We need to go east to reach Swag Island."

Maddox nodded and turned the wheel to the left just a little so the ship turned slightly to the east. It was midday, and the sun was high. It was difficult to tell the direction from the sun, but Tristan consulted his compass.

He looked up at the horizon and pointed.

"There! I think I see land!"

"Is it Swag Island?" Maddox asked eagerly.

Tristan consulted the map and the instruments on the helm. He shook his head. "I don't think so. We have several leagues to go. I think it's Raucous Island."

"Oh. We could stop there for the night and sleep in a real bed in an inn," Maddox said. "We have all this pirate treasure in the captain's quarters. We could borrow some."

"But it belongs to good people," Tristan argued. "We should try to return it."

"It would take ages to return all that gold."

"We could just sail around and give it to those who need it most."

"Good idea. We could give it to some of the villagers on the island when we get there."

Tristan thought about it. "But we're also poor and hungry, so we need it, too. So it's okay to take just a little."

"Right. Come on."

The boys descended the stairs to Fearsome Boney Blaze's former chambers, which was really just a grand sitting room piled high with treasures of all sorts. There were diamonds and rubies and emeralds and coins of solid gold.

The boys had already discovered it, but they were still dazzled by the extensive, glittering heaps of pirate booty Captain Blaze had pillaged from the poor, desperate villagers of the islands.

"How much should we take?" Maddox asked.

"Only so much as we can carry without being weighed down," Tristan suggested. "We wouldn't want to sink because we became too greedy."

Maddox nodded.

The boys scooped up only as much gold as they could carry without being too greedy.

Tristan tucked the coins into his special pocket, and Maddox zipped his into the small pouch on his belt where he kept his special odds and ends.

When they'd taken only what they needed, they marched back up to the bridge.

In the short time they had been in the captain's cabin, the steering wheel had turned just slightly off course.

They weren't concerned; Tristan could still see the tips of the trees on Raucous Island, and Maddox took the helm to turn back in the right direction.

"We aren't far off course," Tristan said confidently. "We will make it to the island in no time, as long as the waters are friendly and the wind doesn't turn."

But the waters weren't friendly. At least, what was under the water wasn't friendly.

As they drew back toward the dark shadow on the surface, they realize too late what it was.

As had happened so many times to unwary, unfortunate sea-travelers, eight huge, purple tentacles burst up from under the water and crashed down upon the Fiery Fatality.

The force of the monster's grip broke the ship right in half, and Maddox and Tristan dove to the side to grip the sinking railing.

"Oh, no!" Maddox cried.

He knew this creature that rose so suddenly up from the darkest depths of the sea and had taken countless ships back down with it.

"It's the Kraken! We have to save the ship!"

Tristan looked at him incredulously. "It's far too late for that. The ship is destroyed!"

The tentacles thrashed and writhed around the hull of the ship.

The masts crashed sideways into the water, splashing the boys as they clung to the railing, swaying and sinking down into the dark, churning surf.

The two halves of the broken ship began to tilt and fill with water until they were sure to sink right down with the giant squid.

"What have to abandon ship, or we will be pulled down with the monster!" Maddox cried.

They met each other's gaze and nodded. They did not spare a moment to fret or fear for their fate.

They both jumped down into the water at the very same moment.

They splashed down into the dark, cold water, and when their heads broke the surface they grinned at each other, for they had survived a very dangerous jump without even a scratch.

A rusty red plank of wood floated past them, and the boys clambered onto it where they could float safely away from the ship.

They breathed in relief and kicked their legs to spin around to watch the giant squid pull the remains of the Fiery Fatality down into its lair in the darkest depth of the sea.

"Well, it was fun having a pirate ship for a while," Tristan said as they spun back toward Raucous Island.

He kicked his legs like a propeller to shoot them forward across the water.

"Yeah, but it was a lot of work, too. I wouldn't want to have to sail the seas all the time, worrying about whether or not the Kraken will come and sink us."

"Well, it did come and sink us, and we survived, so I guess it wasn't that bad."

"It was a very exciting adventure, even though now we have to figure out how we're going to get to Swag Island without the schooner or the Triumph."

Tristan wasn't worried.

"I think we'll figure it out. We've done pretty well so far for our first adventure."

"Imagine how good we will be on our next adventure."

"I guess adventuring is a lot like sword fighting," Tristan mused. "You need a lot of practice to get really good at it. Otherwise, it's just beginner's luck and you could really get hurt."

CHAPTER FIVE

Raucous Island

It was getting late, and the sun was beginning to dip below the glittering horizon when Tristan lifted his hand and pointed straight ahead.

"I think I see land up ahead."

Maddox had begun to nod off a little. Now he lifted his head to look.

"Thank goodness. I'm getting tired and hungry. Have you got anything to eat in your special pocket?"

Tristan sighed. "No. Just the map and some gold, but it will buy us something to eat and a place to stay when we get to land."

Maddox shook his head sadly. "All that treasure just sunk. It's a terrible shame."

"I took note of the coordinates on the instruments just as the monster pulled the ship under. We can come back for it with more men and try to find it under the water."

"It'll be a long way down by then. I don't think anyone has the equipment for that sort of thing."

"We can find a way. Maybe James will know what to do."

"We'll just have to find Bertha's long lost treasure and help everyone on the islands so they won't starve."

"Good idea. Let's paddle to land. It's not very far. We have to get that treasure and get home before we can think about how it can help everyone."

"Yeah, and we'd better take care of our immediate problem first."

It was a long time before they reached Raucous Island, but they paddled hard and never stopped because they knew the giant squid was still out there, and they were hungry and tired.

The sun had nearly set when they finally washed up on the shores of Raucous Island. By then, the boys were soaked and exhausted.

When they looked up, wiping the salt water from their eyes and trudging out of the surf, they found that they had washed up in a small village.

As twilight approached, the people of the village were coming out of their homes, ready for a night of rabble rousing and trouble-making.

Tiny lights glittered all over the village, and it was so noisy, the boys couldn't even hear themselves think over all the racket.

There was a group of men shoving and shouting at each other in the streets between the small shell huts all around the village.

The boys glanced at each other.

When fights like this broke out in Port Scanty, the boys always jumped to the rescue to break it up, but they were so hungry and so tired, they didn't pause to see what all the fuss was about.

"Should we help them?" Maddox asked, but he didn't sound very enthusiastic about it.

Tristan sighed. "We have to get something to eat. Then we can come back and break it up."

Maddox nodded. "Good idea."

There was small inn called the Warped Bottom. It was as noisy as the streets, but it was the closest place to find something to eat in the village.

The boys squared their shoulders and strode confidently into the inn.

They were the youngest boys there, and the patrons looked up at them with cagy eyes.

They studied the boys for several moments, but then they saw their swords and how wet they were, and they nodded in respect and turned back to their grog.

Maddox and Tristan trudged up to the publican.

The publican was a large, bald man with tattoos all over his body so that they could barely see anything of his face but his dark, scary eyes.

He looked down at them in surprise as they approached him.

Then he narrowed his eyes in disapproval. He didn't like kids at his inn, and these boys were tracking in mud and salt from the sea without even wiping their feet.

"What are you two doing here?" he demanded. "How old are you?"

"We're eight," Tristan told him proudly.

"We fought Fearsome Boney Blaze," Maddox explained. "And took his ship, the Fiery Fatality."

After Maddox said this, the whole inn quieted down to listen to the rest of his tale.

"But the ship was sunk by the Kraken," Tristan added.

Everyone gasped and ooh'd and aah'd over their exciting adventure as they recounted how they had been captured by Blaze's crew and fought them to steal their ship, which was now deep in the bottom of the ocean.

Then they told them how they had escaped the Kraken and paddled for many hours to shore and that now they were very hungry and tired.

The publican enjoyed their tale very much. He grinned with his black teeth and slapped the rough wooden bar with a huge hand. "A tankard of grog on me!"

"Thanks," Maddox said. "But we're only eight."

"We don't drink alcohol," Tristan added.

"How about some root beer, then?" the publican asked and slammed two large, frosty mugs on the counter.

The patrons laughed and converged upon the boys to pat them heartily on the back for their bravery and daring.

They appreciated the admiration, but they were still extremely hungry.

"How about something to eat?" Maddox asked.

The publican nodded happily. "How about some delicious Jerk Chicken? It's the house specialty in the Caribbean."

"Is it spicy?" Tristan asked.

"As spicy as the sea is deep and dangerous," the publican replied proudly.

"We'll take it!" Maddox said.

The publican nodded and ducked into the kitchen. He returned moments later with two huge, steaming plates of chicken.

It was spicy! But the boys didn't mind; they liked it that way.

When they had eaten, they felt much better, and they decided it was time to go back out and stop the fight, just like they had promised.

But they had a new problem they hadn't even noticed because they were so wrapped up in their excellent dinner.

Around them, the inn had broken into a terrible brawl.

The patrons were throwing fists and chairs and some of them were tossing each other all around the room, over everyone's heads!

"Uh, oh," Tristan said, watching the mayhem.

"Should we break up the fight?"

They looked at the fighters, then back at each other. "We will be lucky just to get out alive!" Tristan said.

"These people sure do seem to like to fight. We shouldn't take that away from them, should we?"

"It wouldn't be very polite."

"We'd better just go, then. We still have to make it to Swag Island."

"Okay."

But the boys couldn't get through the thick, rough-housing crowd.

They were jostled around by the big, mean fighters and pushed right back to the bar. Then someone seized them and pulled them into the crowd, and they had to swing their fists and dodge the punches coming at them.

"Tristan, jump up on the table so we can get out of this fight!" Maddox yelled.

"Then what? We'll still be in the middle of it!"

Maddox pointed up at the ceiling. There was a rope hanging from the rafters. It was old and frayed and it probably hadn't been used in some time, but the boys were light and lithe.

"There's a rope!"

Tristan jumped up on the table beside him and looked up at it. "You first!"

Maddox wasn't scared of an old rope and a little brawl, so he gripped the end of the rope and swung right over the heads of the fighting drunk people.

He landed right at the door where he could feel the fresh salt breeze. It felt good.

"Tristan, come on!"

Tristan didn't have to be told twice. He gripped the rope as it flew back toward him and swung over the heads of the fighters.

A man reached for him as he whizzed over his head, but Tristan kicked his hands away and landed at the door beside Maddox.

He breathed a heavy sigh of relief. "That was close!"

"I know! These people sure are rowdy."

"That's just no way to be. Let's get out of here!"

When they burst out into the night air, they looked around. "What should we do now?" Maddox asked.

"We have to get off this island. These people are all crazy. All they want to do is fight all the time!"

They sure did.

As they hurried through the sandy, well-trodden streets toward the beach, the people of the island--men and women alike--leapt upon each other with curses and shouts of rage.

Maddox and Tristan didn't even consider breaking them up; if they were enjoying themselves, the boys had no right to stop them. Not to mention, they weren't even sure even their skills were a match for such rage.

The people were like berserkers!

The lights of several large boats twinkled on the beach. It was quieter here than in the village, as most of the sailors must have been on shore leave, but there were a few men tending to their boats at the end of a long sailing day.

They didn't notice the boys.

"There," Tristan said in a low voice, lest they attract the sailors' attention.

He pointed to a small, inconspicuous boat floating merrily between the larger ones. It was not much, but it was seaworthy, and it was all they could have hoped for or expected at a time like this.

"I don't think anyone will miss it," Maddox said, smiling broadly, for he was ready to leave this terrible island.

"It's stealing," Tristan said doubtfully.

"But we need it. We can leave some gold behind. It will probably be worth more than the boat, and the owner can buy a new, better boat."

"You're right. Without it, we'll probably never get to Swag Island and be stuck on this Raucous Island forever."

"Everyone is too drunk to notice anyway," Maddox added.

Tristan scoffed. "Adults. They're always making bad decisions. I'd like to stay a kid forever."

"Yeah. Being a kid is awesome," Maddox agreed. "Adults never get to have adventures like this. They have to stay home and raise kids and work and worry about money and stuff."

Tristan tugged on his arm. "Come on! Let's go before someone sees."

"Okay!"

They ran stealthily through the sand and ducked between the huge ships surrounding the tiny clipper. They could hear the sailors shouting to each other on the ships around them, and their hearts pounded a little.

Even though they planned to pay for the boat, it still felt like stealing, and they didn't want to get caught.

"We have to be quick and very quiet," Tristan whispered.

Maddox nodded, and they pushed the clipper into the waves as quietly as they could and clambered inside.

"Hey, thief!"

Uh, oh. One of the sailors had spotted them!

"That's Blue Eyed Billie's boat!" another sailor shouted.

"You can't take that!"

But they had no choice. They had to have Blue Eyed Billie's clipper. The sailors shouted angrily at them, jabbing their fingers accusingly.

The boys felt very bad, but it was their only way off the island!

Bullets whizzed in the air past their heads as the sailors tried to shoot them. They narrowly missed the boys and the boat and splashed into the water.

"Hurry!" Maddox cried.

Tristan didn't need to be told twice. He took the ores and gave them a mighty row to send the boat skimming quickly across the water away from the indignant sailors.

Maddox rose to his feet and tossed several gold coins onto the shore where they clinked together and shone in the twinkling lights from the ships.

"Payment!" he called, cupping his hands over his mouth so the sailors could hear them. "It's not stealing if we paid for it! We're not thieves! We just need this boat to get home!"

The sailors tried to pursue the boys, despite the payment, but they were not quick enough. Their ships weren't prepared to leave the port yet, and the boys' new clipper was as speedy as James' schooner.

They were gone, into the darkness and away from the drunken Raucous Island before any of the other crews could even leave the shore.

Maddox sighed and took one ore from Tristan to help him row. "Do you think we left enough money?"

Tristan grinned. "For this thing? You left them plenty of gold. Now they can get a ship as big as those sailors or a whole fleet of these little clippers."

"Oh, good. Now we can get to Swag Island and get that treasure." He leaned back against the hull and sighed. "The skeleton pirates are gone, and the Kraken has already sunken one ship today. It will have gone back down into the sea to tally up it's booty from the ship. It's smooth sailing ahead."

The light of the day was nearly gone, but Maddox and Tristan rowed hard and well, and Tristan guided them to land before the sun dipped completely below the horizon and night descended across the sea.

The clipper banked on the shore, and the boys dragged it up onto the beach so the waves wouldn't wash it back to sea.

It was so dark now, and the boys were so very tired. They looked around for an inn, but there was no village at all on their side of the shore.

In fact, it seemed as though this might be one of the uncharted, uninhabited islands of the Caribbean.

They didn't mind too much. It was better than Raucous Island. It was balmy and warm, and there was no one to bother them.

The island was as quiet as Port Scanty as night fell, and it was very peaceful.

"We should find a place to sleep," Maddox suggested as they trudged wearily over the dunes.

"We could sleep under the stars," Tristan replied. "It is very warm, and our coats will keep us safe."

They didn't have to search long. There was a copse of trees along the beach. They had large green leaves like ceiling fan blades.

Some of the leaves had fallen beneath the trees so that they formed a soft blanket upon which the boys could settle comfortably.

"This will do nicely," Maddox said, throwing himself down on the jungle floor and sighing contentedly as he leaned back on the spongy blanket.

Tristan sighed, too, as he lay on his back. It wasn't as nice as his bed at home, but there were worse places to sleep.

"It's been a very exciting day."

"Yeah. I hope James told our moms and dads what we're doing so they aren't worried about us."

"I hadn't thought about that. It's been so hectic, I barely had time to think of anything at all! I hope they aren't worried." He frowned a little. "If James didn't tell them, and they are worried…we'll be in for big trouble when we get home."

This didn't sit well with Maddox.

"I sure hope we aren't going to be in trouble. We're doing a great deed for the Woeful Islands. That should count for something, right?"

"Well, maybe we should have told them before we left."

"There wasn't time." Maddox shrugged, which caused the leaves beneath his shoulders to shift a little. "There's no use worrying about it now. If we can bring back the treasure and save the village, our moms and dads will forgive us."

"You're right. We just have to succeed on our quest and not let worry about the future get in the way. We don't want to make any mistakes."

They were quiet for a moment, contemplating their parents' reaction to their sudden departure.

The night was quiet and still, and it was easy to forget about it for the moment.

From under the canopy of trees, the boys could see the stars shining brightly in the dark blue sky.

Maddox pointed toward a constellation he knew from school. "Tristan, look. There's Pegasus."

Tristan looked to where he was pointing and saw the Great Square with a leg off the bottom and the tilted head.

"I see it." Moments later, he nudged his friend. "And look! There's Cassiopeia."

They pointed out more of the constellations they knew, which was many because their school teacher, Mr. Borealis, loved the stars and was always telling them about the Greek myths and the constellations.

Their favorite was Orion because he was a great warrior, and he was also one of the easiest constellations to find.

They pointed out some of the others they saw: Cepheus, Aquarius and Capricornus.

They had learned them all in school and could name them all night long, but they were so very, very sleepy and the night was so warm, and the leaves were so soft.

They needed their rest if they were to begin their journey anew in the morning.

They closed their eyes, and the sound of the waves crashing gently on the shore and the soft hum of wildlife in the trees around and behind them soothed them to sleep.

CHAPTER SIX

Mambas, Lions and Crabs

The brilliant sun awoke them in the morning, glaring through the trees to let them know it was time to get up and get moving.

Maddox sat up as the warm rays shone on his face, but he froze as he looked up at the trees above his head. "Tristan," he whispered.

His friend was still sleeping, wrapped in his long black coat, but when Maddox said his name, he slowly opened his eyes.

"Don't move," Maddox ordered.

Tristan turned his eyes to his friend, but he didn't move a muscle. "Why?" he whispered back.

"There are four snakes right above your head in the tree."

Tristan rolled his gaze to the leaves above his head, and he saw what Maddox meant.

Four bright green snakes hung from the branch right above him, staring down at him with their beady black eyes. They hissed as though they knew he was watching them now.

Venom dripped from their long, sharp fangs.

"What are they?"

"I think they're green mambas," Maddox said. "But they live in Africa. I don't know what they are doing here."

"Maybe some traders or pirates brought them over on accident or to sell them or something."

"That might be why there are no people on this island. They might have gotten them all to pay them back for taking them away from their home in Africa and forcing them to live in a strange place."

"That's not really important right now," Tristan whispered. "What are we going to do with them?"

Maddox reached for his sword slowly so the snakes wouldn't become nervous, for he knew green mambas were a very nervous breed that attacked quite aggressively when they were in danger.

He wasn't slow enough, though.

Two of the snakes snapped their heads up to look at him.

Then, suddenly, one of them launched itself from the tree and flew directly at his face!

Maddox whipped his sword through the air and sliced the angry mamba's head right off.

As though he were enraged by his brother's death, another snake flew out of the trees toward Maddox, but Tristan was much quicker.

He drew his gun and fired.

The dead mamba landed beside his equally dead brother.

The other two snakes did not take their brothers' deaths lightly!

They dropped out of the tree right onto Tristan's head!

Before they could bite him, though, he seized their long, thin, scaly bodies and threw them off. Tristan and Maddox raised their guns and fired in the same moment.

The snakes blew apart as though they had been filled with explosives!

Maddox heaved a sigh of relief, and Tristan wiped the sweat from his brow. They looked at each other and grinned. "Whew. That was close!" Maddox said.

"Yeah. Those snakes almost got us."

Maddox bent down to pick up the poisonous green bodies at their feet. He held them up and grinned at his friend.

"Hey, Tristan, what do you think?"

Tristan smiled back at him. "Breakfast!"

The boys carried the snake bodies to the beach and found some sticks to rub together to start a fire.

When the dry, crumbly driftwood was burning steadily, they skinned the snakes with their knives and speared the meat on a spit to roast them over the flames.

When they were good and roasted, they pulled them off the spit and tucked in.

The snake meat was a little rubbery, but it was pretty good, and they didn't like to waste the animals they killed, even horrible venomous snakes planning to bite them.

"These are pretty good," Maddox remarked, chewing on the last of his mamba's tail.

"Yeah, but they would have been really good with barbecue sauce," Tristan replied.

"Or that Caribbean Jerk we got at the inn last night."

"But you have to make do with what you have on a deserted island, I guess."

After breakfast, the boys splashed around in the waves for a while, as they loved the water even after they'd experienced so many dangerous adventures on it in the last couple days.

They weren't ready to start out on their voyage again.

They were brave and daring, but they were still eight year old boys.

They needed a little fun and relaxation from time to time without all these adult responsibilities on their shoulders.

The island was large and wild, and there were many adventures to be had.

They hunted around for two large, thick walking sticks. When they found two perfect sticks, they headed into the thick jungle, which was noisy from the wildlife that had awakened with the day.

They couldn't see any of the creatures, though. They must have heard of their defeat of the wicked green mambas because they steered clear of the boys tromping through the jungle flora.

But as they reached the crest of a hill, they saw a large, tawny cat stalking through the trees ahead. They looked at each other in surprise.

"Is that a lion?" Maddox asked.

Tristan squinted his eyes to see it a little more clearly. It had a long, fluffy mane and a long tail.

"I think so."

"What is it doing here?"

"I don't know. Lions live in Africa, too. Maybe it came over with the mambas."

"Someone was very irresponsible with these animals. They do not belong here. Creatures shouldn't be taken from their homes and left somewhere where they are a stranger and all alone."

"I agree."

The lion paused as though it heard their voices and turned toward them. For a long time, it studied them.

Its mane was thick and fluffy, and they knew it was a male lion. He was probably lonely, but his dark eyes looked mean and hungry.

"What should we do?" Maddox asked.

"Leave it alone and let it pass," Tristan suggested. "It is a dangerous beast; we don't want to fight it unless we have to."

Maddox agreed, but the lion didn't seem to have the same idea.

After several long, silent moments, he must have decided the boys were a threat to his territory or that he had to prove his status as the king of the jungle.

He lifted its head and roared so loudly, the boys' hair blew back from their faces.

They did not wait to see what he had in mind; they drew their swords and guns and readied them for his attack.

He charged at them with another fierce and mighty roar.

They fell back as he leapt at them. His paws were as big as their heads and his claws as sharp as razors.

As those huge paws flew at their faces, they both fired their guns at the same time and rolled to avoid the enormous, heavy lion, which fell to the jungle floor with a loud thump.

The boys jumped to their feet, breathing heavily, for a lion attack was enough to rattle anyone's nerves

They looked down at the lion, then back up at each other. "Are you thinking what I'm thinking, Tristan?"

Tristan grinned. "Of course I am."

"Lunch!" they said together.

***

The lion was a hearty meal roasted over the spit, but walking around the island and fighting lions had left the boys with voracious appetites.

They also missed their very favorite food: the crabs that scuttled around the shore and in the shallow waves.

On the beach at their home in Port Scanty, the boys would spend hours hunting for crabs and gathering them in huge buckets for the feasts the villagers would throw on special occasions when the crabs were plentiful and the people were not stricken with the many illnesses the poor village experienced from time to time.

As the sky started to darken in the approaching twilight, the boys hunted around the shore for the large crustaceans they liked best.

They were very patient, as one must be to do any sort of fishing, and finally the spotted a family of huge crabs scampering along the shoreline. Maddox jumped into the water and caught one in his bare hands.

Its pincers snapped dangerously as they wrestled, but Maddox held tightly on.

"Tristan, help me!" he said as the large, angry crab wiggled and snapped to get away.

Maddox held on tight and didn't let him go, but the crab's pincers clawed at his face.

Tristan pulled out his sword and sliced them off.

He bent and picked them up before they could wash away because they were the best part!

Tristan threw the pincers into a little bowl they had fashioned from the tree leaves.

The crab flailed helplessly without its claws, and it stopped struggling after a moment. Maddox tossed it into the bowl with the pincers.

Tristan saw another large crab trying to escape, but he jumped on it and held it up to Maddox, who used his sword to slice off the snapping pincers.

The two crabs were so huge, they didn't want to be greedy and catch more than they could eat.

They gathered some water from the sea and boiled it in the leaves over their fire.

The crab's shells made a satisfying cracking noise as the boys popped them open and pulled out the meat.

They tasted salty from the sea water, but they both agreed they preferred their crab with a little butter sauce.

When they finished their favorite crab dinner, they lay back down on their leaf beds and looked up at the stars.

They named their favorite constellations for a while, but they were sleepy from their adventures and full from their exotic meals, and they fell right to sleep before they were even able to find their favorite star, Betelgeuse.

CHAPTER SEVEN

Shrunken Heads and Flaming Dragons

The boys were awakened again by the bright Caribbean sun, but this morning a shadow passed across their faces and blocked out the brilliant light.

The boys opened their eyes at the same moment and looked up into the faces of a gang of men and women dressed in animal furs who stared down at them with angry expressions on their sun-burnt faces.

There were streaks of red paint on the tribe's faces, making them look as though they were streaked in blood.

They were surely headhunters, for their spears were long and sharp and there were stacks of shrunken, leathery heads on the shafts of the spears as though they had speared the heads and left them there as a trophy or proof of their skill.

Some men and women had only a few heads, but others had so many, they barely had room to grip the spears.

Maddox and Tristan suspected they were in big trouble.

They knew for sure when the headhunters threw back their heads and let out a single, blood-curdling shriek like a war cry.

They raised their spears as though they intended to add the boys' heads to their already impressive collection.

The boys were better fighters than these headhunters, though, and so they were not afraid. They drew their swords so fast, the tribesman had no time to retaliate and sliced off the jagged, sharp metal heads of their spears.

The headhunters were so surprised, they stared in awe as the boys jumped up and shoved them backward, knocking them to their bottoms. Then the boys ran.

They pushed their little clipper into the water and leapt inside. The angry headhunters pursued them, shrieking and shouting in a strange, exotic language the boys had never heard before.

They didn't pause to listen or try to understand what the headhunters were saying.

"Hurry! Hurry!" Maddox cried as they paddled frantically away from the shore. "They surely want our heads."

But the headhunters did not want them badly enough to pursue them.

They stood on the shore, shouting and waving their spears angrily.

They did not have a boat, and if they did have one somewhere, stashed in the trees, made of bark or leaves, they did not get it and chase after the boys.

Maddox breathed a big sigh of relief.

"That was close. I didn't know they were there on the island at all."

"They were probably hiding from us because we have guns," Tristan said.

He consulted his map and compass.

"Go west now. The next island we come to should be Swag Island. We're nearly there."

"I am ready to end this adventure," Maddox admitted. "Hunting in the jungle was fun and all, but I am ready to go home and see my mom and dad."

Tristan nodded. "Yeah. Me, too. And I want to sleep in my own bed. Sleeping under the stars is nice, and we get to use our knowledge of the stars to entertain ourselves before falling asleep, but I like to be under my own covers instead of sleeping out where headhunters are watching us."

They both sighed. They were silent as the boat floated serenely away from the island they had decided to call Shrunken Head Island.

They didn't know what it was really called, but that's what they remembered most clearly about it, even though they had had many great and excellent adventures there and enjoyed themselves greatly.

Though, they did have to admit that hunting lions was the most fun they had had in a very, very long time.

***

In the distance, a land mass rose above the horizon. A line of trees swayed in the gentle, sea breeze. It was thick with green foliage. Tristan pointed excitedly.

"There it is! Swag Island! We're finally there."

Maddox grinned and they paddled the boat toward the landmass. In moments, they slid aground on the shore.

The island was quiet as Shrunken Head Island had been, but they knew the dangers of an ostensibly quiet island.

Anything could be hiding in the caves and trees, ready to jump out at them at any moment.

"This place seems deserted," Tristan said hesitantly after several moments of scanning the shoreline and the trees beyond.

"The coast is clear today," Maddox added.

They were excited to finally find the lost treasure and complete their marvelous quest. Tristan consulted the map for several moments under the hot, glaring sun.

He laid it out on a large, flat rock on the edge of the shore and looked around. He pointed at the big red X, then looked up and all around.

"The treasure should be right around here," he said, frowning thoughtfully.

They scooped up the map and looked around them. An outcropping of rock lined the shore, just like on Kismet Island, and the boys knew that the rocks might not be exactly as they appeared.

"It must be here somewhere," Maddox said, peering closely at all the rocks for a cave mouth.

"Yes, probably in a cave somewhere."

"But I don't see a cave."

Just as Maddox said it, he leaned against one of the larger rocks, and it moved, startling them both. Tristan strode over to it and shoved on the rock.

As he did, it rolled away from a large, gaping cave mouth.

"It's here!"

They looked at each other a little grimly.

"I'm not sure how I feel about this, Tristan," Maddox said. "You remember the last time we went into a cave. It was very bad."

"Well, this time we scattered all the skeleton's bones in the ocean. They won't be coming back to bother us."

Maddox nodded. "You're right. Let's go, then."

The boys marched straight into the darkness of the cave.

Tristan handed Maddox a flashlight, and they switched them on, casting their lights around at the walls and the passage ahead.

There were no cave markings on these walls. They were just plain stone grey.

They trudged eagerly through the narrow passage, which was barely tall enough for them, excited to finally have reached the end of their long, arduous and dangerous journey.

"This is a strange place to hide a treasure," Tristan remarked. "Only a very small person or a child could get through this cave."

"It's lucky we're the ones who came," Maddox agreed.

"Do you think James knew all along that he wouldn't be able to get the treasure himself?"

"Maybe. Maybe he came to us because he knew we were the only ones who could do it."

They considered this in silence as they strode along the passage.

Suddenly, a huge, dark shape reared up in front of them. They couldn't tell what it was, but it roared so loudly, the cavern walls shook.

Tristan and Maddox stopped in their tracks and drew their weapons. Tristan cast his light at the huge, dark shape and they realized immediately what it was.

It was a huge, black bear standing on its hind legs. They didn't know how it stood in such a low area, but it must have been standing where the ceiling was higher.

It didn't move to attack them.

"Why isn't it attacking?" Maddox whispered.

"Maybe it can't move," Tristan whispered back.

"But it can go down on all fours and the ceiling won't be too high for it."

"Maybe it's not real."

Maddox frowned thoughtfully. The boys looked at each other and stepped bravely forward to discover the truth.

As they did, the bear roared again. It was louder than the lion's roar had been, not because the bear had a larger voice but because they were in such a small, narrow space.

This time, as it roared, the boys felt its breath blow their hair back.

"Nope," Tristan said. "It's real."

But as they moved closer to the bear, it still didn't advance toward them.

They inched closer.

The bear swiped its claws angrily at them. The boys stopped and looked at each other.

"Maybe it isn't moving because it's guarding something," Maddox suggested.

"The treasure!" Tristan exclaimed. "What should we do?"

Maddox thought about it a moment then nodded decisively. "I'll distract it. You look for the treasure."

"But what if it gets you?"

"I will be okay. I am strong, and I am not afraid."

Tristan nodded. "Okay. Be careful, though! It is a mean and dangerous creature."

"I know. When I distract it, you have to hurry."

"Okay!"

Maddox drew his sword and approached the bear. He was brave, and so he was not scared of the mean bear.

He didn't hesitate at all.

He swung his sword at the huge animal. The metal clanked against the bear's sharp claws as the bear defended the strike.

The bear swiped at him again, and this time he lifted his sword to meet the bear's claws.

While Maddox did this, Tristan crept forward and ducked past the bear.

The animal roared angrily at Maddox, and Tristan's hair blew back.

And then, suddenly, Tristan dropped right out of sight!

"Maddoooooooooooox!"

Maddox was almost distracted by his friend's plight, but he raised his sword to defend himself as the bear struck out at him again.

"Tristan! Are you okay?" he called.

"Maddox! I found the treasure!" Tristan's voices sounded as though it was coming from directly beneath him.

It echoed in the cavern, and Maddox knew he must be in a wide space.

"It's down here! It's all here! There's a staircase, too. But you will have to get past the bear."

"I can do it!" Maddox exclaimed.

"There is another passage down here. I think it leads out. Hold on. I see light."

"I'm a little pressed for time here!" Maddox called back as the bear swiped at him and he protected himself. "Can you hurry it up?"

Tristan's voice came back again as though he was moving closer very quickly.

"There is a passage! It goes out to the beach! Come down here!"

"Coming!" Maddox swung his sword at the bear.

As the bear lifted his claws, Maddox leapt up and kicked the bear right in the mouth! The bear roared plaintively and stumbled backward.

Maddox darted past it and jumped down into the opening Tristan had fallen through.

"Wow!" he exclaimed as he landed on his feet beside his friend.

The cavern in which they stood was small, but it was very tall and there was a treasure chest right in the middle of the room.

The chest was filled with gold and huge rubies, diamonds, emeralds, and sapphires. There was a beautiful gold necklace with large jewels of all colors.

"Wow!" Maddox said again.

"My mom would like that necklace!" Tristan said.

"My mom would like this gold crown with the jewels," Maddox said

Tristan turned to Maddox with a grin. "We found it! We finally found it!"

They gave each other a triumphant high five.

"Now we have to get it back on the clipper," Maddox said. "Do you think we can carry it?"

"It is heavy, but it is not too heavy for us. We are the strongest boys on the Woeful Islands!" Tristan told him confidently.

They closed the lid on the chest. There were handles on the sides of the chest, and they each took a handle.

They lifted together, and it wasn't too heavy for them, as long as they helped each other.

They were eager to end this adventure and show James and villagers what they had done to save them.

They hurried up the passage toward the light from the beach, which was dazzling the closer they drew.

They had not felt so exhilarated in a very long time.

When they emerged onto the beach, back into the light of day and the fresh salt air, a line of skeletons waited for them with their swords drawn.

They were dressed like pirates, and their clothes were even rattier than before, as they had spent much time under the ocean, reforming and rising back up to the surface to find the unfortunate boys.

"Oh, no!" Tristan said.

"They must have gotten their bones back together!" Maddox added.

Fearsome Boney Blaze was standing beside their small clipper on the shore behind the row of skeleton soldiers.

As they watched in dismay, he bent down and touched the flames of his head to the small sail--they didn't know how he had gotten lit back up, but his fire was as deadly and dangerous as ever!

Their little clipper went up in flames so quickly, the boys had no time to race to its aid.

Fearsome Boney Blaze laughed wickedly.

"Oh, no!" Tristan said again.

"Our ship!" Maddox added.

Then the skeleton pirates rattled wildly and attacked.

It was all the boys could do to fight them off, still holding onto their hard-earned treasure each in one hand.

They broke the skeletons apart as easily as ever, for the pirates' skills and strength had not improved after their stint submerged in the ocean water.

They kicked the bones far and wide apart so it would take them longer to put themselves back together.

"What are we going to do?" Maddox asked, kicking a skeleton pirate's skull all the way into the water where it rose and fell with the crest of a wave. "We have no ship! Boney Blaze lit it on fire!"

"We have to take theirs!"

"But how? Blaze will get to us first."

"We beat him once," Tristan reminded him. "We can do it again. He was foolish to come back for more after the sound beatings we have given him."

They did not drop the chest, but they let out a terrible war cry and rushed toward Fearsome Boney Blaze with their guns raised.

They fired rapidly at him, but the crazy old pirate merely laughed and flamed. He barely seemed to notice they were shooting at him, for the bullets just seemed to bounce right off him or through his boney ribcage without even striking him.

He must have kept those rum bottles somewhere in his capacious coat for just such an occasion, for he drew them almost as quickly as the boys fired.

He lit them all with the flames coming out of the top of the head and hurled them with deadly accuracy toward the boys.

They shot them out of the air, and they exploded in a shower of sparks, glass and liquid. They rained down on the heads of his crew, but they seemed not even to notice.

"Shoot his eyes!" Maddox suggested.

His eyes were glowing blue furnaces, and they were easy to see.

The boys aimed their guns as they ran toward him and fired all their bullets into the fiery holes in his skull.

The bullets rattled around in his empty, flaming head for a moment, but when they tried to get out the other side, there was no way out.

They simply carried Fearsome Boney Blaze's head right off his neck!

It landed right in the surf. The surface of the water bubbled and steamed as the head sank into the waves.

They boys roared in triumph, but they knew it wouldn't be long before Blaze and his crew put their heads and bodies back together and came after them again.

"That should keep him down long enough for us to take his ship again!" Tristan declared. "Let's go!"

They raced across the shore, kicking sand up from their boots as they did.

Fearsome Boney Blaze and his crew had acquired another terrible looking ship with rusty red sides and a raggedy flag with the captain's flaming head.

They heaved the chest up onto the deck--for they would not for a moment let it go, as they knew it was what the pirates really wanted--and leapt up onto the deck after it.

On the shore, the skeleton's bones were beginning to rattle and join back together.

"Hurry!" Tristan ordered Maddox as his friend took the helm.

"I'm hurrying! I'm hurrying!"

He spun the wheel to steer the ship toward the horizon. They just had to get home with their treasure and everything would be all right.

It wasn't alright yet, though.

Just ahead, spots of fiery red were approaching from the distant horizon.

They frowned at them in bewilderment for several seconds as the shapes moved closer and closer.

They realized what they were moments too late. Maddox lifted his hand.

"They're dragons!"

But they weren't just any dragons.

Like Fearsome Boney Blaze, they were flaming skeleton dragons, though their entire bodies were covered in flame, not just their heads.

They were gaining on the stolen pirate ship, and they looked as though they intended to run right into it!

"I've never seen anything like that before!" Maddox exclaimed, lifting his finger to point.

"Me neither and I'm pretty sure Mr. Borealis never mentioned them."

"Where did they come from?"

Tristan squinted around. Then he pointed. "From over there!"

There was an island ahead, but it wasn't like any island they had seen before. Smoke rose from its shores, which were nothing more than scorched, glassy sand from the volcano in the center of the island.

The volcano spewed lava all over the island around it. The lava ran red hot down the sides of the big stone rock and spit flames into the air.

The whole island appeared to be on fire!

"That explains where they came from and probably where Boney Blaze got his flaming head," Tristan added. "But that's not really important right now! We have to turn the ship or they are going to hit us!"

Tristan was right, but they were too late!

"There's not enough space to turn!" Maddox cried. "We're going to hit the island!"

As he said it, the ship crashed into the smoldering shore, and they were thrown down onto the deck.

A lick of flame struck the ship, spat from the volcano's hot, gaping maw. The ratty sails ignited instantly.

The boys knew they would be in trouble if they didn't get off quick!

They each seized a handle on the chest and leapt off the ship seconds before it suddenly exploded in a fiery inferno.

"Oh, no!" Maddox complained.

"This must be Fearsome Boney Blaze's home," Tristan said thoughtfully.

He hopped aside to avoid another flaming ball of lava, which smoldered where he'd been seconds before.

"It's dangerous here."

"Maybe the dragons are his pets," Maddox suggested.

The boys shivered as they thought about this.

"Flaming dragon skeletons would be awesome pets!"

"Except you can't ride them because they are on fire," Tristan replied.

"Yeah, that's true." Then Maddox lifted his hand to point. "And here they come!"

"And there's Boney Blaze!"

The Fearsome captain of the Fiery Fatality was swooping down upon them, riding astride the flaming dragon, whose eyes were huge jewels of ruby flame.

The loyal beast must have reignited its master, for Boney Blaze's head was back atop his shoulders and burned with as much rage and heat as ever before.

His flames shot up so high, they could have almost touched the soft, wispy clouds above his head.

The dragon swooped down toward the shore as though it meant to scoop them up in its sharp, flaming red teeth.

They ran to avoid it as it dove at them.

At the same time, they dodged the flying lava and licks of flame that fell around their heads and threatened to burn them right up.

They narrowly escaped the dragon's teeth and the balls of flame. In fact, Maddox felt the very tips of his blonde hair singe in the heat as a fireball whizzed over the top of his head.

The dragon crashed into the volcano ahead, but they knew it wouldn't keep Blaze and his fiery mount down for long.

"What do we do?" Maddox asked his friend, for Tristan always had a plan.

But Tristan's quick thinking wasn't going to save them so easily.

They skidded to a stop before several huge piles of bones. They weren't human bones, for the bones themselves were so big, they reminded the boys of the museum displays they had seen in books of long dead animals like T-Rex and his brothers.

These dragons must have been of the same species, for their bones were as big and they had probably looked a lot like them when they had still been alive.

The bones were still and chalky white from the sun beating down upon them day after day, but the boys knew better than to trust a seemingly inactive pile of bones after all their adventures.

"Oh, no!" Maddox said, backing away from them. "Do you think they are going to come to life?"

"It seems to be the thing to do around here if you're a skeleton," Tristan replied grimly.

As soon as he said it, the volcano spit another stream of lava, and a fireball landed right in the middle of one of the piles of ancient dragon bones.

The pile burst into flame and flew up into the air, joining into a perfectly shaped dragon skeleton.

It waved its flaming head around as though it were trying to wake itself up.

Maddox considered it for a long moment. "Maybe we can ride it."

Tristan looked at him incredulously. "It's on fire!"

"I'm not afraid," Maddox told him confidently. "I think we can find a way. They might help us off this island."

He stepped toward the flaming dragon.

Tristan wanted to protest, but he knew his friend was brave and he would be all right.

Maddox put out his hand as he approached the dragon skeleton like a dangerous dog.

"Hello," he greeted him in the soft, comforting voice he used when one of the neighbors' dogs escaped from their owners and needed to be brought home.

"Hello, Dragon. I won't hurt you. I'm a friend. We just need your help."

The dragon's fiery gaze settled on him as though it could understand his words. It didn't move.

"Will you take us home safely from the skeleton pirates?" Maddox asked.

The dragon regarded him for several long, still moments.

Maddox and Tristan didn't move, either, because they knew if the dragon decided not to help them, it was a very dangerous foe indeed.

Maddox stared into the dragon's fiery eyes.

Finally, the dragon lowered its head in a sort of big, dragon nod. Then it dropped down on its haunches as though it expected them to hop up on its back.

Maddox grinned and stepped forward to touch its head, but its body was too hot, and the flames were too high.

He sighed.

"I can't touch you. You're on fire." He glanced at his friend. "I'm sorry, Tristan. I tried. I don't know what we're going to do now."

Suddenly, the dragon rose up into the air behind him. They weren't sure how he could fly without his leathery wings, for they were just bones, but he could.

He rose higher, and then he shot away from them. The boys watched him sadly, and for the first time since they started their journey, they began to feel fear for themselves and for their village.

The dragon hadn't abandoned them, though! He had agreed to help them, and he was a loyal friend.

They watched as he swooped down into the churning sea and emerged seconds later. He smoked and sizzled, but he wasn't on fire anymore.

Maddox pointed. "Tristan, look!"

The dragon circled the island once in pure joy of being alive again and dove back to the shore to land beside the boys.

"We can ride him now!" Tristan said, grinning.

Maddox walked toward the dragon and smiled. He patted his huge, boney head.

The dragon made a rattling noise that sounded almost like a cat purring.

"Do you think you can carry this chest?" he asked.

The dragon lowered his belly on the sand. The bones of his vertebrae were flat, and they would hold the chest quite well.

The boys heaved the huge, heavy chest up onto the dragon's back. It barely seemed to notice the extra weight.

Maddox gripped a jutting piece of bone on the skeleton animal's neck and swung himself up onto its back.

Tristan looked at him in dismay.

"With the chest on his back, I won't fit!"

Maddox leapt back down onto the sand.

"I can't leave you here. You take the chest back to the village and the dragon can come back for me."

But Boney Blaze and his dragon had discovered their whereabouts, and they were nearing the island!

"But Boney Blaze is coming!" Tristan said, pointing. "You have to hurry. You take the chest!"

"No! You will surely be in trouble. I will stay and fight with you."

Their new friend, the dragon skeleton, had something else in mind, though. He opened his mouth and breathed a thick, dark puff of smoke at the other pile of bones beside which it had once lain.

The smoke smelled of sulfur and sea water.

It smelled exactly as they thought brimstone would smell.

The boys didn't wince or hold their noses--it wouldn't be polite.

The pile of dragon bones sprung suddenly to life, as though their dragon's breath had awakened it. It smoked and smoldered, but it did not ignite into flames.

Their dragon made a strange sort of noise as though he was speaking to the other, and the new dragon bent down to allow Tristan to swing onto his back.

The boys grinned at each other and hung on tightly as their new mounts rose up into the air.

The wind rushed at their faces, and their hair blew back.

It was scary to be up so high, swooping and circling over the water, but the boys clung to the dragons' vertebrae and they did not fall off.

"To Port Scanty!" Maddox cried into the wind. "In the Woeful Islands!"

Their dragons turned together and raced through the air toward their home. They were faster than any ship, even faster than the legendary ships in tales of pirates and soldiers.

But they were not faster than the flaming dragons upon which Boney Blaze and his crew pursued them!

The flaming dragons and their riders were gaining on them. "Look out!" Tristan yelled.

Their dragons evaded their flaming foes, but the pirates' dragons were relentless. They chased the boys and their new friends through the air, keening in terrible, rattling rage.

"We have to fight them!" Maddox called to his friend.

"How do we fight flaming dragons?" Tristan asked.

But their dragons knew.

They suddenly swooped down toward the water, and the boys had to hang on for dear life so they wouldn't fall right off!

The dragons opened their jaws to scoop the seawater into their mouths. When they rose back up, they faced their enemies and spit the water right out into the flaming dragons' faces.

Fearsome Boney Blaze bellowed in rage as his dragon sizzled and went out.

His own head fire sputtered and finally died.

He looked small and not very fearsome at all anymore.

"Yeah!" Tristan shouted.

"Awesome!" Maddox added.

Their faithful and clever mounts spun in the air and flew at the enemies, snarling and snapping their huge jaws around Boney Blaze's dragon's ribcage.

The dragon skeleton broke apart in mid air and tumbled toward the churning waves.

They heard Boney Blaze's angry shouts as he plummeted into the ocean.

Then they heard a loud, satisfying splash.

CHAPTER EIGHT

Two Prodigies Become Ordinary Boys

Maddox and Tristan would have many adventures with their new pet dragon skeletons and fly to countries no one in the world had ever seen or even heard about--not even James or Mr. Borealis--but that is a story for another time.

James was waiting for them, and their village was still poor and starving.

The treasure they held would save them all, and they could not put off their return home any longer, no matter how worried they were that their parents would greet them with angry faces and a litany of admonishments.

They steered their dragons home, despite the thrill and exhilaration of their flight.

When they landed on the shores of Port Scanty, the whole town came to watch the enormous skeletons descending on the glittering sand with the two boys astride them.

They had never seen such a spectacular sight as the skeleton dragons or known such brave, dashing and heroic boys as Maddox and Tristan.

When the boys alighted on the beach, their mounts laid down on their haunches to rest.

They did not know if dragon skeletons slept, but they knew their new friends would wait for them until they were ready to join them on new adventures.

The boys patted the dragons' heads and turned to greet the villagers who rushed to them with hugs and warm greetings.

They looked around for James. He was pushing through the crowd with a wide grin upon his face.

He looked as though he had been weary and worried, for there were dark circles under his eyes.

His face was red with sunburn as though he had spent many days on the shore, watching for the boys to return.

"Did you get the treasure?" he asked.

The boys nodded eagerly and dropped the chest they carried between them. They flipped open the heavy, carved lid for all to see.

The gold and jewels glittered in the sun, nearly blinding the onlookers who ooh'd and aah'd over the immense, beautiful treasure.

James was delighted.

"There is enough here to save our village and all the villages around the Woeful Islands! You boys were very brave and impressive. Thank you so much for saving our village!"

The villagers surged forward to admire the treasure, and Maddox and Tristan joined James as he gave them each a piece of magnificent gold or a huge, glittering jewel.

The treasure was so grand and so extravagant, and each piece was worth so much money, everyone in the village was now rich instead of poor.

Maddox and Tristan handed out the treasure, and they smiled as all the villagers thanked them and cried in happiness and relief over their sudden good fortune.

No one in the village would ever go hungry again, and they were not greedy.

There was plenty of treasure left over for the other villages around the islands that had been pillaged and plundered by the wicked pirates.

The Woeful Islands and their neighbors would be saved for many years to come.

But when all the villagers had taken their treasure, Maddox and Tristan looked around for the people they really wanted to see.

Then they saw them.

Their moms and dads were waiting for them on the crest of a dune, smiling and waving at them.

They had never been happier to see them in their lives, and they couldn't wait to tell them all about their adventures and the adventures they would have in the future.

Their parents were so happy to see them, they even forgot the boys had frightened and worried them and didn't even mention a single punishment.

They hugged them for so long the boys thought they would suffocate!

Maddox's mom loved the jeweled crown, and Tristan's mom loved the beautiful sparkling necklace.

They cried tears of joy, and they never even scolded the boys for leaving without telling them.

That night, the whole town had a huge celebration to honor the boys and their good fortune.

They ate fish and crab and delicious vegetables just harvested from the farmers' gardens.

Later, as the boys lay in their beds in their own homes, they thought of all the adventures they'd had and the dangers they'd faced.

They couldn't wait to get back out and see the world with their new pet dragon skeletons.

But just for that night, with their mothers and fathers sleeping in the rooms beside theirs, they were happy to be home in their own warm beds.

There would be more danger and more adventure for these brave and daring prodigies, but just for tonight, they were happy to just be average, ordinary boys.

THE END

www.ingramcontent.com/pod-product-compliance
Lightning Source LLC
Chambersburg PA
CBHW070638130626
46555CB00006B/2606